The Prince and the Witch

Written by

Marianne Hesse

Illustrated by

Angela Paul

Marianne Hesse

The Prince and the Witch
Copyright © 2024 by Marianne Hesse

All rights reserved. This book or any portion thereof may not be reproduced or used in any manner whatsoever without the express written permission of the publisher, except for the use of brief quotations in a book review.

Printed in the United States of America

Illustrations by Angela Paul
Graphic design by Claire Flint Last

Luminare Press
442 Charnelton St.
Eugene, OR 97401
www.luminarepress.com

LCCN: 2023924201
ISBN: 979-8-88679-465-6

For Roy Edwin Hitch, John Myers,
and Berthold August Leonhard Hartrich,
three princes among men.
—Marianne Hesse

For Shan,
a great friend and a great motivator.
—Angela Paul

I, for one, was born in the castle.
Dignitaries attended my birth.
I, firstborn son, resented the title
that sat on my head like a curse.

If I ran down the hall,
cracked a vase with a fall,
my tutors would all have a fit.
Yet women would curtsy,
men groveled for mercy,
it surely made me want to spit.

Simply said, since I was rich,
I asked, at once, to see a witch
then insisted we be left alone.
I said, “Dearie, you must hear me out.
Now lean in close, don’t make me shout.
I need to find a new home.”

“Although I’m prince of all you see,
it doesn’t mean a fig to me.
In truth, what good is it for?
If I can’t sing a salty tune
or swing a rat or mock a loon,
why would I stay here anymore?”

The hag held up her bony thumb.
She smirked and said, "Esteemed young one,
with sense you would stay where you are.
But since you're prince of all we see
and want to go, well, change with me.
Given your wealth, I'd go far."

Now who could give much thought to that?
A crooked nose, an old crone's hat?
No thank you, that wasn't my style.
"Make me something else," I said.
"Long on fur, humongous head.
Ferocious, yet able to beguile."

"Come on, change me!" I demanded.
"It would not be underhanded
to do whatever I decide to decree.
I'm the prince, I'll have my way,
and you must do whatever I say.
I'm in charge, so now you'll listen to me."

Without a sound, the hag drew near.
Her fetid breath made my eyes tear.
A cold wind blew as though it came from the sea.
She screeched, "I, alone, will have my way,
and you must do whatever I say.
Servility, you'll see, will be owed to me."

Her darkened eyes grew full of scorn.
She cursed the day that I was born.
Her cruel mouth oozed a vile and green sticky foam.
She sneered, "So you want out of here?
You'll get your wish and then some, dear."
Never had I felt so scared or alone.

Her shadow loomed upon the wall.
It grew in stature, ghastly tall.
Her thunderous voice scared me so, I held my breath.
Her body swayed, she mumbled low.
She moaned, intoned, how could I know?
The spell she'd weave would seem a fate worse than death.

"Abracadabra, royal birth
or wealth won't tell him what he's worth.
Abracadabra, let him squirm.
Still the palate will crave worm.
Abracadabra, malapert
No one escapes their just dessert."

My forehead suddenly felt damp
then both my legs began to cramp.
I shook my legs, glanced at my toes.
I gave a shout, a croak arose.

Could I deny my feet were green?
Not only green—webbed in between.
I gave a shout,
another croak came out.

The old crone pointed to the door
and crooned, “See you don’t scratch the floor.”
She gave me a cold, toothless grin.
“As prince, no doubt, you’d still belong,
but frogs and such had best be gone.
Don’t dawdle, foul amphibian.”

To hop away with style and grace,
this princely frog faked one brave face.
But if the truth be told, my head was bowed.
Now some might say, “Son, show some pride.”
How could I? Green and scared inside,
I hopped away but under a dark cloud.

Vanquished out into the sun
made me feel a tad undone,
her cackle filled the air as I hopped away.
Let her cackle, let her gloat.
Shove that croak back down your throat.
What choice did this frog have but to obey?

Dumbfounded, I pondered
alone, one grim frog
forced to leave home for the stench of the bog.
The witch flew away, a sly grin on her face,
leaving me lost in my fear and disgrace.

I looked atrocious.
Eyes bulged from my head.
If only I'd wake from this nightmare in bed.
I prayed for relief
and I croaked out in vain,
"Don't go, don't go, change me back again!"

But how can one stop an old crone who's departed?
Being a frog is not for the faint-hearted.

Out in that relentless sun
without a pocket, on the run,
I longed for my scepter and crown.
The bog, the swamp, the bugs, the heat,
the muck that ebbed at my webbed feet
had turned my whole world upside down.

Slumming in the summer sun
was not, for me, one bit of fun,
unlike those other frogs who seemed content.
I, for one, was not amused.
For pity's sake, I had no shoes.
Long days of catching flies seemed so misspent.

Sipping green slime in the pond
reminded me of days beyond
my reach, when I sat dry upon my throne.
Through days of unrelenting heat,
how many flies can one frog eat
until he feels abandoned and alone?

I prayed that someone would appear
who'd find my frog face quaint and dear.
Some princess wandering in the murky bog?
And why should I not be sought out?
I was no scoundrel, fool, or lout.
With hopeful heart, I peered into the fog.

Perhaps she'd say, "What have we here?"
Kiss my frog face and shed a tear.
Of course, she'd come, how could she stay away?
My spirits rose, I felt them fly
to meet my dreams, caress the sky.
Waiting for her kept my fears at bay.

I sat up nights, I dragged through days
of dreary unrelenting haze.
Yet not once did that princess come to me.
Why should I not be sought out?
Was I a scoundrel, fool, or lout?
Didn't I deserve to be set free?

"Am I more than the bugs I eat?"
I asked myself in dark defeat.
I rued the day I called that witch to me.
If I could turn things back, time-wise,
of course, I would apologize.
I'd been a fool not to have let things be.

A fool, alone, would think it wise
to mope and overdramatize,
demanding that the crone do things his way.
Who but a dolt would deem it right
to tell a creature of the night
that she must follow his rules and obey?

When all my hope began to ebb,
someone caressed my slick green head.
I jumped a foot—now who'd be kind to me?
The old crone cackled at my start.
Her face, though ugly, warmed my heart.
My webbed feet itched to think they'd be set free.

The witch, of course, had cause to gloat.
My croaks, like dumplings, clogged my throat.
On wobbly, bended knees, I croaked my plight.
"I'd rather sit upon a throne
than in a pond, wet, all alone.
How could I be so wrong and you so right?

"By wanting something else," I cried,
"I lost my throne, my crown, my pride,
rejecting what the fates once gave to me.
While peasants dream of being kings,
I wished to be other things.
I lost sight of all I was meant to be."

Once I professed my shame and plight,
the witch set out to make things right.
She told me she was pleased with how I'd grown.
In the time it takes to twirl a globe,
with seaweed dangling from my robe,
she plucked me from the pond back to the throne.

An easy feat, no doubt, for that old crone.

Epilogue

Now that all is said and done,
the prince would prove the lucky one
in spite of what the witch had put him through.
No longer thinking he knew best
made him wiser than the rest.
He gave grave thought to all he'd say and do.

When finally back upon his throne,
still a lad, a tad more grown,
he better served his subjects, kith, and kin.
Having been both prince and frog,
bored on the throne, thrown in the bog,
had made a prudent ruler out of him.

He ruled with both his mind and heart,
no longer feeling torn apart,
wishing to be something he was not.
His subjects hailed him as they should.
For he was noble, wise, and good—
no longer that young, brash, smart-mouthed upstart.

Life deals out uneven hands.
We're prisoners of shifting sands
and of fates that tell us who we are to be.
Yet in that framework, where we find
ourselves, of course, we can be kind
and kindness will most likely set us free.

For in that framework, large or small,
from lowly worm to prince so tall,
challenges, no doubt, will come one's way.
So whether we are nobly blessed
or more or less like all the rest,
we still determine how we'll meet the day.

About the Author

Marianne Hesse

The Prince and the Witch is Marianne Hesse's fourth children's picture book. The first three, *Then We'll Say Goodnight, That Bird on My Plate,* and *The Fishers' Tale* were also done in collaboration with illustrator, Angela Paul.

About the Illustrator

Angela Paul

Angela Paul is a concept artist and illustrator from Germany. Her illustrations have appeared in the children's books, *Then We'll Say Goodnight*, *That Bird on My Plate*, and *The Fishers' Tale.*

To see more of Angela's illustrative work,
visit her on Instagram:
@vilblue

Printed in the USA
CPSIA information can be obtained
at www.ICGtesting.com
JSRC081408070224
56623JS00008B/11

* 9 7 9 8 8 8 6 7 9 4 6 5 6 *